W9-AWQ-273

All Through My Town

Jean Reidy illustrated by Leo Timmers

BLOOMSBURY
NEW YORK LONDON NEW DELHI SYDNEY

First published in the United States of America in March 2013
by Bloomsbury Children's Books
www.bloomsburykids.com

For information about permission to reproduce selections from this book, write to
Permissions, Bloomsbury Children's Books, 175 Fifth Avenue, New York, New York 10010

Library of Congress Cataloging-in-Publication Data
Reidy, Jean.
All through my town / by Jean Reidy ; illustrated by Leo Timmers. — 1st U.S. ed.
    p.   cm.
Summary: Illustrations and simple, rhyming text take the reader on a tour around town.
ISBN 978-1-59990-785-7 (hardcover) • ISBN 978-1-61963-029-1 (reinforced)
[1. Stories in rhyme. 2. Neighborhood—Fiction. 3. City and town life—Fiction.] I. Title.
PZ8.3.R2676All 2013   [E]—dc23   2012023304

Art created with acrylics
Typeset in Billy
Book design by Donna Mark

Printed in China by C&C Offset Printing Co., Ltd., Shenzhen, Guangdong
(hardcover) 10 9 8 7 6 5 4 3 2 1
(reinforced) 10 9 8 7 6 5 4 3 2 1

All papers used by Bloomsbury Publishing, Inc., are natural, recyclable products
made from wood grown in well-managed forests. The manufacturing processes
conform to the environmental regulations of the country of origin.

To Mike, my wingman on all my adventures,
whether they be halfway around the world
or just around the town —J. R.

For Gina, without whom I would be lost —L. T.

Rising, waking.
Bread is baking.
School bus honks its horn.

Seeding, sowing.
Rooster crowing.

Counting ears of corn.

Pancakes flipping.
Cutting, clipping.

Tossing, fetching,
bending, stretching.

Brushing, shaving.
Good-bye waving—

my town in the morn.

Shopping, sacking,
sorting, stacking—

rows so nice and neat.

School bells ringing.
Reading, singing,

friends to meet
and greet.

Starting, stopping,
trolley hopping.

Blazing, dashing.
Red lights flashing!
My town's busy street.

Stamping,
mailing,
painting,
nailing,

ladder up and down.

Whistling, wheeling,
helping, healing.
Laugh away a frown.

Shelving, shushing.
Fountain gushing.

Swinging, lunching.
Cookie munching.

Peeking, peeping—
someone's sleeping . . .

All through my town.